Minecraft: Diary of a Wimpy Kid

Table of Contents

The World Can't Handle Me!

Ever had the feeling that the world can't just handle all the requests you have? No? Yes? Not sure? Well, if there's something I am sure of that is precisely the fact that the world just can't handle all the requests I have. The world can't handle me! I am asking too much, you might think or even say it out loud, but that, my friends, is just not the fact. I am everything but needy. All my requests are decent. I asked from my mom and dad to buy me a game I heard about. I just want to spice up my days and make the world a little less boring.

am awfully bored and expecting the game any day now. Hopefully, the game will arrive today! I did my part of the bargain and had my grades made all straight A's. Well, not all...my parents agreed that my B in Math is not much of a big deal. So, I earned my game fair and square.

Also, I had to clean my room and do another round of chores so I could seal the deal with my parents. The game is expected any second now, any second now...

KNOCK! KNOCK!

That must be my mom knocking on the doors of my room. The game is here! I just hope she doesn't take a look at my closet. She won't think my part of the deal is done if she sees my sock drawer.

"Feel free to enter my Kingdom, mom!"

I love being dramatic just for the sake of having fun.

Plus it makes me sound super awesome; also

making me feel like I am really a king and my room

is my castle.

"Hello, honey..."

My mom entered. She was looking around my room

and I knew that she was actually checking if I had

everything tidy and arranged in accordance with

our house rules. One of the rules was: No food on

the floor.

I think I at least got that one right if nothing else.

She finished with checking my room out. The whole situation looked like I was under some kind of investigation and she was a tough de4tective looking to crack the case.

It didn't match my kingdom fantasy, but it was kind of fun. Detective Mom had nothing on me and I could sense that she had my present somewhere with her.

"All right, honey...", she smiled as she was putting on her I APPROVE face. I liked that face. It meant everything was all right. Things were going in my favor and it felt good.

"Mom?"

"Yes, honey?", she was about to leave but I stopped her at the doors.

"Are you forgetting something?", I was full of hope feeling my eyes glowing in suspense.

"Oh, yes…", she said, handing me the game.

MINECRAFT!

"All right! Thanks mom!"

"You are welcome, honey. Your father and I forgot the game's name so we really had troubles finding it, but we eventually did   it successfully."

Forgot? Mom, come on, who can forget the name of the best game ever??? I don't even know how that's possible.

Of course I didn't say that. I just thought about thinking about saying it. I am confused by this sentence, so we will all move on and forget that I just said that.

My own copy of Minecraft was with me and my mom was already at the doors leaving my room and her own approval. My mission was completed! And another mission was about to start.

"Oh, and honey…"

"Yes, mom?"

"Take care of your sock drawer, honey. I know what's in there…a mess…", she smiled and left.

I think all mothers are a part of some secret agency where everyone knows everything. It makes sense, right?

Sock Drawers and Zombie Mowers

So, I opened my copy of Minecraft and placed it where it belonged! I my CD room! The game started and I picked the world. It was awesome. Did you know that there are thousands and thousands of different worlds in Minecraft, and you can end up anywhere?

There can be a snowy biome, desert biome, forests, lonely islands...

The chances are that you will never get to end up in the same place more than once, so I warmly recommend you save your game if you like it.

There's also a biome with giant spotty mushrooms. I bet one of those mushrooms would make an awesome shelter. You could dig your rooms inside of the mushrooms and make sure you are 100% safe in there.

Nights can be unpredictable and harsh in Minecraft, so I bet it's important to find your way around.

Oh, I just got the island biome! Awesome! I think there's nothing here but trees and a house...strange looking house...but, oh well...it still feels like an adventure.

I just have to grab some snacks and I am on it...wait, what is this?

I stepped on something and I thought I did a fairly good job with cleaning my room.

It was a cube...and it looked like something you would see in Minecraft. It looked like a block and it was only one inch big.

It had something sticking out at the other end...

I checked and saw an extension that looked a lot like something you would see on an USB driver.

Hmmm, maybe it came with my copy of Minecraft.

Maybe some kind of an extra edition for my game...

I decided to check what it is, so I placed it there

where I would naturally place my USB drive.

Nothing...

I stood up as I remembered that my mom asked me

to take care of that sock drawer of mine before I

start with my game. I knew she would check on it

soon, so I'd better take care of it now.

That is when I heard a strange noise. It was an uncommon case of growling I have never heard before.

I turned around and saw that the game was on. That little cube sticking out from my computer was glowing!

I don't remember I saw it glowing before...

I approached it and touched it...I felt my entire body trembling and crackling as if I was made of...blocks...

Before I knew it, I was sucked into the game! My toys and posters on the walls were turning into sky and sun with edges, the walls were turning into trees and the floor was turning into sand blocks.

I was surrounded with ocean! I was IN THE GAME!

I was living Minecraft, not just playing. I wasn't sure how this happened, but I loved it!

I could still hear that sound of growling. I wonder where it was coming from and what was the thing making that sound.

Oh...I just remembered that there are Zombies in Minecraft. I wonder if it's a Zombie I hear growling...or maybe more...oh, no. What am I going

to do?

The sun is slowly setting down and I have nothing

on me. I better start cutting trees or something.

What will I use for cutting? There's nothing around

me but trees and flowers...and yes, there are apples

around. But, I don't think apples could save me

from Zombies.

They don't look or sound like craving for apples. I

could maybe throw apples at them...maybe not.

I started chopping trees with my hands. Apparently you can do that here. No logic in there, but hey – I am not rebelling against it. It's kind of cool. Actually, it's awesome.

I managed to chop enough wood for a crafting table – you need to make that first in order to be able to make super awesome tools you can use for defense and all sorts of things, like mining and digging.

Yes, I know everything about Minecraft although this is my first actual time in the game.

Still confused about how this happened.

Plus, I am not sure how am I going to get back. My sock drawer was still a mess and if I am not back in my room when my mom returns, I will have a lot answers to give. And I really don't know how to explain all this...

For now, I have other things to worry about – like for example: not to get eaten by that growling Zombie. This growling makes him sound like a truly hungry mob, which is probably the case. I am not planning on ending up as someone's lunch.

I made myself a really cool sword.
Huh? What do you think?

It looks good, right?

GROWL! GROWL!

Looks like I have a company! It's a Zombie, all

right...and yes, he has a Zombie friend.

It's time to check how my Zombie Mower works.

Yes, I named my sword Zombie Mower. I think it sounds pretty cool.

So, as much as I hoped I won't be an interesting apparition for Zombies, they were heading right towards me and I didn't like it.

I was forced to use my sword. I closed my eyes and started swishing with it.

It took me some time to get rid of them. Once the growling stopped, I took courage and opened my eyes.

Closing my eyes while swishing my sword was probably not the greatest idea, but I guess Zombie Mower did a wonderful job.

There, where two Zombies were growling at me just a second ago, was now a piece of rotten meat waiting to be collected.

Yuk! Rotten meat sounds bad enough as it is, and I have to carry it around with me.

Anyways, I decided to take it and store it...maybe I will need it for something. Who knows...

The Boy Who Cried Wolf

It seems like there is nothing around this island except for one wolf I am constantly seeing around.

There is also one small house that looks more like a cottage. I still didn't get the chance to check it out, but since I didn't make my own shelter yet (yes, that might be a bit irresponsible on my end, since I really need to get a shelter).

That wolf I was watching approached. It seems like he was watching me as well. He approached in a strangely friendly way – it was like he was waiting for me to give him something.

I don't remember I owed him anything, but then again I didn't want him to eat me. I don't want to believe that everything these mobs have in mind is eating me.

He sure looked like he was waiting to be fed. He looked like my dog, Spotty, when he start waving his tale and looking at you with expectation in his eyes. You would know he is hungry when he does that.

I had a couple of apples I was saving for when I start losing my energy, but I don't believe apples would come as interesting to a wolf, although this is a game.

I offered him an apple. He refused it. Well, of course. That is when I remembered that I had that piece of rotten meat6 with me. It's rotten, but he might like it.

Still better than apples to a wolf, I suppose.

I offered him the piece I had and he accepted it! What do you know? He loved it! I think he now thinks we are friends as I see a strange case of hearts floating above his head.

I guess that is a clear sign that he likes me. He was following me everywhere I went. I guess I know have a pet wolf and he likes rotten meat.

I think we have lots of Zombies to conquer with my Zombie Mower to feed Wolfy!

Yes, I named him Wolfy. I don't care that the name is too obvious and not at all creative. I like it and Wolfy doesn't mind.

There's No Place Like Home

So, although I managed to make myself a lovely shelter just for the sake of being protected during nights around here — I wasn't sure for how long was I going to be stuck here — I still decided it would be a good idea to check on that cottage or shack or whatever it was. Maybe the shack belonged to someone and maybe that someone could help me get back to my world and play Minecraft as every other normal kid: outside of the game and not the other way around.

Wolfy and I approached the house. I asked him to wait for me outside while I take a look around. He wasn't happy about it – at least he didn't look happy – but he obeyed anyways.

I knocked on the doors a couple of times, but no one answered.

I thought trough the situation for a couple of moments, and then I took the liberty to enter the shack uninvited.

The shack was fairly small as it seemed as it was made out of a single room, but it really looked nice and neat.

Everywhere you looked there were books and bottles...I think the bottles contained potions. I am not sure. It seemed as if there was lots of brewing going on here, so I presumed those were all potions.

"Don't you dare touch any of those potions! As ignorant as you are, you would pick the Potion of Harm."

Huh?

I turned around and saw her:

It was a witch! I forgot about them. Did you know

that all Witches were once only Villagers, but once a

Villager gets stroke by a lightning, it turns into a

witch and gets really good at Brewing?

You now know.

"I am really sorry...I was just..."

"You were sniffing around. That is what you were doing and that is probably what you would go on with if I hadn't appear."

I was a bit scared, I had to admit. She could throw a potion at me and hurt me with it. I knew potions were very powerful. I wish I got the chance to learn more about making potions.

"I'll be on my way now...", I was trying to get out of the awkward situation, retreating and walking towards the exit.

"I apologize again…"

"Well, don't you want to find out how you can get back home?", the Witch said.

How did she know that??? I was amazed and stunned at the same time. I suppose being stroke by a lightning had its perks after all. I wonder if I get to turn into a witch if I get stroke by lightning.

Probably not. Most possibly not. I would probably lose my energy and…GULP…die.

"Well, yes…that is exactly what I would like to find out…I am really sorry for intruding…I knocked but no one answered…"

"I heard you knocking, but there is no way I am ever in the mood for company…Anyways, I will let you know how to get back home…"

"Thanks!"

"You didn't let me finish, boy…"

Oh…I bet the rest of the sentence doesn't sound so good.

"I will reveal the secret of your return home if you agree to bring me something from the underwater Temple…"

"There's an underwater Temple around here?"

"Of course there is…I wouldn't agree to live on a deserted island with no fun around, would you?"

"All right, I agree…what am I looking for?"

"I need the Eye…"

"The Eye?"

"You will know it when you see it….trust me."

I don't know why I agreed. I am not sure, really. It

didn't sound safe at all, but I really needed to get

back home.

The Eye and I

Wolfy was once again following me everywhere until we came to the edge of the seashore and I dipped my feet in the water.

The water was warm and nice, but I couldn't stop myself from wondering what kind of mobs will I have to fight to get that Eye for the witch and assure my return home. What if I mess everything up and end up here forever? What if I get slain and don't get the chance to re-spawn?

Everything was a huge, massive WHAT IF.

I said my goodbyes to my faithful friend Wolfy as I didn't know when and if I was going to be back. He was howling in sadness, but he still couldn't go with me.

I started to swim, diving constantly as I was trying to spot the temple. How hard could it be to find a temple?

Swimming in the game was awfully difficult but I was somehow finding my way around.

And that is when I saw it! The temple! It looked magnificent:

All of a sudden and completely unexpected, the temple started turning into my desk with my computer on it and the water around me started to turn into the walls of my room. I saw familiar toys and posters.

I was home!

But how?

That is when I saw my mom. Oops!

She paused the game and was looking at me angrily.

"Ahem! Your sock drawer? I thought we agreed you should first take care of it and then start your game..."

"I..."

I was confused and thought I'd better save the truth for myself. My mom would probably think that was the worst excuse anyways.

"I will take care of it..."

"Right away, honey!   Chop, chop!"

Chop, chop...Hah! That made me remember the first time I chopped a wood in Minecraft.

"Right away mom, of course."

I guess the Witch will have to wait for that Eye...the game was on Pause, so I don't think she will notice I took a while with searching for the Eye. I wonder what the Eye serves for. It must be something ultimately awesome – it sure sounds awesome.

But, my next adventure will have to wait until my sock drawer is all set up.

Manufactured by Amazon.ca
Bolton, ON